White Van

I0662444

Meg Tuite

Unlikely Books
www.UnlikelyStories.org
New Orleans, Louisiana

White Van

Fifteen Dollars US

ISBN: 979-8-9851371-5-6

Library of Congress Control Number: 2022931553

Unlikely Books

www.UnlikelyStories.org
New Orleans, Louisiana

"I'm convinced nobody on earth writes with quite the same level of passion, verve, candor, dark humor, electric intensity, and heart as Meg Tuite. I've pronounced this collection my favorite of her works (and I have a bunch of them). Why? It's the experience of reading it. You read the first sentence. Stop. Read it again. Shake your head. Read it out loud. Marvel. Feel. Look out the window. Read the whole tiny piece (a poem? a story? you've long since stopped categorizing these stunning mash-ups). Whisper: *damn*. You gasp, you sigh. You read more. You start to gobble these. You mark ones to go back to. Realize you've marked them all. A master, a maestro, Tuite is the kind of writer who can balance a jetliner-sized story on the tender tip of a blade of grass and not you or I or anyone else has a clue how she does it."

—Kathy Fish, author of *Wild Life: Collected Works*

"The poems in *White Van* grind and seethe, they crawl from the backseat of the van down the block. With a withering tension, Tuite circles the globe of abuse, trauma, and memory, repurposing abduction as an inquiry into the psychosexual damage inflicted bodily upon young women. This is a hammer-hard voice, decisive in its ability to smash together the tragic and the familiar, the familial and the societal, the languages of both predator and survivor. A raw and urgent collection, steady in its honesty, as present in its performance as a siren."

–Colin Pope, author of *Why I Didn't Go To Your Funeral*

"Estranged bowels, ghost bones, mirrors, blades—*White Van* boldly confronts womanhood, the body, our insecurities and oppressors. Meg Tuite's words will trap you in this winding, suffocating yet cathartic ride. It cuts right to the heart and is impossible to look away."

—Lucy Zhang, author of *Hollowed*

"Meg Tuite takes us into the dark hallways of American life with this harrowing, incredible collection of prose. Women, children rise to rattle the walls, rub fire into the 'cold cases.' Pronouns shift, images scald, memories glimmer near 'some shrieking puck of a moon;' a blanket, a pillow, a muffled scream. This book ruptures the silence with language that holds a knife between its verbs. 'We rock handjobs and blowjobs in the dark from boys who buy movie tickets,' Tuite writes, and we are left to wonder if the price of entry for women in this country has always been too much, too much. A monster of a book for the silence of the monsters in us. I can't recommend it enough."

—Alina Stefanescu, author of *Dor*

"*White Van* is in Tuite's terms a 'predarectomy'—the removal of the predator. The book follows the 'endless line of girls' who have 'stepped here before. She never realized how easy it was to disappear.' We climb inside the white van and come face to face with terror: the serial killer rapist— his family—his victims and the writer who is able to create conflict, action, and resolution in each scene. A story must parade in this order across the well-eaten page. This is exactly what Tuite does—each chapter is its own seamless chilling narrative—and we are there with the speaker riding inside the white van, a witness to evil. 'Blood on paper is a bad joke,' but this collection of fiction and poetry is both remarkable and disturbing. *White Van* is a book you can't put down, a book you will forever remember."

—Anne Elezabeth Pluto, author of *The Deepest Part of Dark*

"Tuite's *White Van* is a work of startling lucidity. She captures the myriad frightening, familiar figures who stalk lunch counters and verge on small town edges in masterful language. This is an elbow to the mouth, a merciless howl in the face of a world given up on the Disney version of fairytales. Tuite's characters persist in the reveries of the loner. She knows her beat, this appalling world of solitary pathos. It is a starkly eruptive world of words beyond death, beyond decay."

—Clementine E Burnley, speaker and writer

"Gorgeously brutal, jaggedly mattering, Meg Tuite's incantations crackle with the clarities of a true visionary. *White Van* treats the trample and grime of trauma with cleansing ecstasies of language. This book will turn you inside out."

—Garielle Lutz, author of *Worsted*

WHITE VAN

CONTENTS

Death Every 3 Seconds

Streets yawned thick with floundering old men, bellies tethered to slant.

Lips drooled and eyes, well they were askew, like there was sun to squint through.

It was night and dogs were wailing at the wind.

Someone was going to die tonight. Maybe not someone known to go out, but men were watching porn on the Sabbath and nautical calendars were getting sloshed.

A man walked through streets wondering if his penis was impressionable because it had soared up and swept into another man's mouth, while his tightened wife was searching for parsley to layer on top of their pork roast. She did love the look of her greens. They rasped and scrambled for sky until she guillotined necessary overachievers into a rich lack of disparity.

Two instincts were recoiling when a girl was told the chemo was unsuccessful, when actually it had spent a year rolling her toward the tomb. Her estranged bowels had insisted that she quit her job and leaf through a buried life of broken clocks, toilets, and herself. Wasn't there another place to search?

He realized he was shaking more and his right hand wouldn't do what he said. Soon gravity called him by name and his body was underwater with rippling skin swaying on waterlogged feet. His dance was violin-shaped as the world bent under his weight. The hollow tracks of his bones loosened the streets. The sky was red and swollen. He was peopled with gestures that did not bury themselves.

The pork roast, satin in its pink skin, waited for the knife.

I DON'T LiKe THiS GaMe

Let silence charade this derelict house. First Communion sits in front of me for three days. Sores on Mom's arms won't zip up. Shake her clammy leg and she pets me. Go get some cake, hija. I sleep, eat, kneel in the white dress. Our last room quaked with fire spires. No candles, I say to the cake. How many años, bonita? asks the man on a couch. His shoes straight black, shiny, offer a hand. Don't touch that cake. I need to get to church. You have a car, Mister? White van slides shut. It matches my dress.

Remember What?

We walk the streets of cities. We run through subways and catch trains to somebody's house, not ours. We stand outside liquor stores and badger strangers to buy us beer. We lay out at a beach laden with old men in speedos and hard-ons. Guys in windows expose their dicks and we laugh. No one touches us. Every day, after school, is adventure. We beat each other up. Boy versus girl. Over and over. Winners end up going steady. The guy produces a piece of shit ring for one of us to wear. We disappear. We steal rings from shops.

Home is where black and blue resonate love. We don't talk family. That is for pathetic girls who hang on to charred childhoods as if we aren't rage peeled away. Step back. Give us another beer. We'll tell the story. That man in the park we call a tumor in our throat flutters as he knocks us to our knees and grips the back of our heads behind the bushes. Others under lampposts while their friends watch.

What happens en route to wherever? Jacked up on jizz and angel dust. Guys with vans rack up surf; drown-pelt-sog our faces with the spit of them. Now there, snitty girls. We'll throw you out, easy as dumping an empty can. Go home to Mommy and nighty-nights. Quick with your 'nos' and tremoring silent tears. Hedging your bets on aftershave aching bores who saturate the sheen of protection and adoration. Not here, bitch.

We rock handjobs and blowjobs in the dark from boys who buy movie tickets, while they stiff like company banging out another night of 'faster, faster' whacking their junk into cinema.

Handfuls of girls disappear over the years. Cops call them 'cold cases' when no one gives a shit.

We crack beers and idle around the dead. That one was a smear of memory. She winnowed through footsteps and chitchat. Another was an inferno from her screened window. Her body was discovered three weeks later under a batch of leaves off a backroad.

"Fuck that," we say. "Those girls were already on their way out," says one. "Waiting for Daddy to save them," says another. "They didn't even know what to look for." We nod. Ram into each other in the van and stare out into moving blurs that pass us.

ROCKS AloNg The BoTTOM

A few low lamps mimic some kind of shrieking puck of a moon. It pierces. Greenery outside is sharp, sways, but gives nothing of its pockmarked façade. Transient shapes crumble walls inside. A siren blackens the wind every few minutes, skimming off the past.

Look for me among the surface of those who swallow days. We drive as though there's a place in wait. The phone rails somebody's face on a screen. We used to have something to show and tell. We drive. Maybe for an oil change. There's free popcorn and no one talks. Maybe we circle the city as though goddamn traffic cares. Always appear as though there's a destination. It's a deliberate way to keep someone from flicking the vulnerability switch of you. Look determined.

 I reside in a house full of holes. Peel its layers of skin. Shards of me expose themselves. Cracked from childhood, a mouth full of teeth shatter in dreams.

I wake up to a face in a mask one night. We both begin to breathe beyond our means. His eyes, his being, as discarded as furniture covered in white sheets. I'm not pronged for the job of 'what color were his eyes,' 'what was he wearing' 'how tall is he' kind of shit. My wrists are bound behind my back with twine to the overwrought sounds of us. He whispers "live or die." Words that cluster through graveyards.

Great sweeps of seconds thread us from control to passive. One for the other. It's a fucking deranged dance. He bores into me. No dew of moisture, though I cry for rain. See my skin. Raised and brayed as a fresh tattoo. I sink bitten fingernails into an island of flesh, break it, break it, but no goddamn ghosts.

I'm not a homicide. I am a homicide. Not in their reports. The mask did what it did and now I'm a paint-by-number girl. I exist in tiny beige squares. A neighbor next door spots the white van and a man in dark clothes. They ask me over and over, "how tall was he", "what color were his eyes", "what was he wearing?"

My sight takes in the yellow tape, uniforms mill, and still I see a crushed version of myself when Mom was alive and cutting my bangs for the school photo in second grade. I worked diligently to wiggle my two front teeth out together the night before the class photo.

You can number the days. How many spent inside not answering the phone? How many peering out the side of the shade? A shower, a toothbrush, another goddamn shirt. "You're not talking," they say.

Sometimes in the morning I can lie so still that nobody remembers me.

This Volcano Is Active

She won't get out of bed.
A bruise the size of bankruptcy
whips the map of childhood
from her ass to the back of her knee
colors of vile tongues
blaze their chatter
secrete in rich hues
not to snarl or disturb
the burn of rash excuses.

Many will want her
with pants that overlay
the thinness of clocks
windows sheer with selfies
cleavage spray and sweat
stink of consequences.

Her body props a website
with child bones angled
as though beaten already
many fantasize they kick.

What happens when an angel
gags dried-up blood

inhales to strangers
wraps them like knick-knacks
around her inner shame.

Sorry. She waits.
Sorry. He comes.
Sorry. Where are you?

FiShiNg FOR FlOaTeRS

Rooms chain together by scars. Invisibles ghost around ghosts. Creaks claw at the entrance, rocking mid-step. Come on, fat day, let up and let us alone. A door-to-door burden of tomorrows skim off hours of heart and lungs for troubled buildings of huddled thought. How is it we soothe each other with a bottomless horde of tasks? Movement decrees a healthy lure of mass indulgence.

*   *   *   *

So much prospect in a childhood of misplaced parts. No one knocks on George's door. Some firing line of desire pulls him out of his trailer. Plans never manifest outside his van. Days crank themselves out through heat. A temperature hits when it's time to go. George answers to no one, can leave or not. He drives and drives until he parks. It is a color, a dimple, or a snotty nose that opens the hatch.

Once he spots the kid, heat accelerates. All now is about navigating the adult. Not one can see her kid through the long hall of activities that siege each day. George knows it will be an easy catch. It always is.

Buried Alive

Locked house. Kids in bed. Parents home. I am writing hazy across four decades. Noises from inside slit the throats of outside. Are those footsteps on the stairs? Prisons are not even a window with a bar away. There's a tiny cubicle under the attic. Say that no one knows about this delicate room, but me. Say that no one knows there's a latch inside that throbs with a keen sense of the lurkers.

Remember. Kids splay out in different rooms. One kid nestles between two walls that touch her. Rustling pages. Flashlight drips words in and out. A blanket. A pillow.
It's when I let safety consume me, I must guard.
And yet, I respond when called. The latch, an embellishment as it slides from its hinges.

DRive-By

Fistful of fear slacks my joints with a tendency to brazen the blood. So many corners in this sweet town of four thousand ruffles call out the riff of fractured boredom. One God-given single lane of circle-rouge girls hop up on strangers and a shift to the benign. A vacant infestation of weed and unconventional fingers encompass a gnarl of simple lust.

Yes, I get in the van parading never-to-return Jane Does of the past. The guy travels reckless stories; gleans the map, top to bottom, as though no one regrets the memory of him. But here he is in my town that anchors ankles like boots on cars. A street meets a face meets a history meets a drug meets a stranger meets the marrow of littered gossip.

A pair of breasts swing beyond the crawling crack pipe. All thumbs aroused and urgent. Six girls giggle and whoop, wait to be plucked by a definitive. I watch the van graze the curb, the window rolls down to my smile. Dimples have mined sparks of Hollywood through jail end horizons. I ask, "You ready to be ripped open by the stars, baby?"

Yeah. I get in the van, smirk at the posse left standing. They are forced to go back to sitcoms, casseroles, and the blank hysteria of Moms. The guy skirts us into the one-lane road of anonymity and hands me a beer. I roll down the passenger window and wave. The sweet landscape slowly starts witching us into deeper green. Soon we nestle in the reserve of jawline forests. The wind is might with wild and threat.

Where The Street
Meets The Body

The body despises itself. There is a sliver of knowledge of the traumas it passed through in these decades. There is no breath. The lungs have a lot to say about what's going on, but are muffled, held mute by the warfare of blazing old trails of pneumonia and bronchitis. Over thirty years later and still it is branded on my lungs. I would never deny anyone their agony. But, no matter how many suns drop into the ocean, life is not finding me any easier to bear. So every time I swallow a cactus of mucus, a jagged breath slashes between the thick bars of prison.

So many skies have bled across my vision. I'm not the type to go to the hospital to tread on my crass lifestyle. I see a collage of skeleton x-rays with Day of the Dead ribbons and milagros rippling across my ribs. It's a goddamn parade.

When I was a kid they put me in an oxygen tent for months at a time. I could barely see people through a wrinkled, thick plastic. What has changed? I've replaced the blurry plastic with endless bottles of wine. This is the splintered parody I have chosen to manage myself within the murky world of adolescence through adulthood. It's another way to suck the life out of the body and keep childhood memories at bay.

How many therapists does it take to remodel the mindset? When do the cravings for escape shrink themselves instead of me?

Right now, the familial infestation is in my gut. The doctor says all of us cart these bacteria around like a second body. Sometimes they attack the host and wreak armies who seek revenge for a quickened leakage toward death. The streets have had free rein to enter me for as long as I can remember. I have sucked on their skin. I have sucked on their bottles. I have sucked on their pipes. They are reciprocating. They are sucking on me.

There is nothing special here. It is as simple as surrender to the paralysis of another day. We are told there are choices. Anything can happen. The strange invitation I read and abide by is much like building a fire to keep the bones warm. I will meld into the fabric that has comforted me. I am tethered to my ghost of yesterday. Somehow he keeps me planted in that strange patch of decimation I call home.

Remove Me from Myself

The blood is a yesterday.
A wrist ought to weigh itself
in rings no bracelet
can navigate.   Allow me
to unhinge fear while hunger
rips open the limbs
of cardboard fat
with Saltine burials.

I hunker in my closet,
a sleeve of fuck yous
in search of bloats
snatched drunk from their trappings.

No table agonizes my appetites.
All scrape and sweep,
No crumb bears the rug
with evidence of fever.

It's a simple recipe.
I swell before a mirror.
Let me tell you I see.

All the sway and banter
of rusty word trash mistakes

me for an audience
of incompetent space.

No. Don't plump up
the adjectives.
My memoir is written.

Flushed and circuiting
the sewers of rabid avenues,
It travels through the city,
like no back alley
footsteps could.

THERE IS a WiND iN THE TRASH

Bottles drunk and faithless frame you. Internal organs swerve slang in stilettos.

No surprise. Inward predation wrestles full gallop. Do your lungs compress into lips,

steam banking random nightmares of mutter-skid skin? A window, jump-full of infections, ugly vomiting scars perch from a white van, creep-sooted toenails, percussive and crusty layer your shins in asphalt.

Tremble scours woman after woman into uniform casts. Tremble polaroids off-road thick with prolific forestry. Tremble graveyards any escape. The map tangles, stains with the blur of blood. Everywhere is semen and the caw of hunger. No surprise. You weather under a pelt of soil and leaves.

EVEN THE LEAVES ARE DEAD

The sky disappears. Trees fill in cloud tremors with savage thoughts begging us to look anywhere but here. Skirting, skirting, skirting away as we lunge forward, two sisters.
"Warm milk morning, noon, and night."
"Crates full of food. Baby blankets."
"Call her Baby."
"Call her Sneakers."
"She's a good girl. Just afraid."
One sister clamps down. "I got her. Hold on. Wait for me."
The other sister turns toward the light. "I'm running home for food."

He moves from city to city, animal shelter to shelter. A huge cage sits in the back of the van wriggling with kittens. His target practice when he was a boy. Now, his practice targets kids. Two girls. Two girls in a forest. Two girls in a forest focus on a kitten. He secures the rope between his fists. This one is long enough for two little necks.

Sister runs. She doesn't notice the man for the vision of the kitten at home, full of milk and food, covered in blankets in her lap.

Can you see it? The girl left behind is eight. Two reveries conspire. One is the kitty and the girl who pets it. She keeps a tight grip and murmurs loving words. Two is the man who comes up behind the girl, snaps the rope taut, and snuffs a gush of desire out of both of them.

Awful Dead I Am

Flowers break their necks in a submerged color pool spewing oranges, yellows, pinks, and reds. Lilies, carnations, roses, and daisies squeeze splinters of life out of this roadside debris.

An awkward package dumps here in the frost one night where cold and quiet buzz blisters through hearts. A sticky gush of secrets choke a graveyard thick with every step. Another muck of creaking virgins bed beneath wilted leaves, shiftless cement, the stirring swell of moss-kempt waters. Girl. Boy. Whose body will it be? Looks to be about the size of a whole lot of inward battering lives that will never open the blinds again.

Knock on a door. The house obeys. Dredges into property of uniformed cops. Family, neighbors, friends sweat and dangle from coat racks at the ready for the call, what, strip, when, swab, why, who, repeat, a cesspit of the culpable. How well do you mourn? God enters; falls inside words and sharpens with each bite. Caution tape gawks and glares at alleged innocence.

Time kisses the cunning fade out of fight. Silent drag-throughs of remember... a long way off since... if only... where the cops now...forgotten...move on...stronger blur each day. Plastic blooms prop-up the landing site with a spray of forever.

Rancid

The drone of it careened thick. A teeming multitude of carcasses smothered a hand over nostrils. Deep layers permeated a whole season of wretched plaque green caverns of tobacco spittoons thawing pustules through this crawling town of 6,173 residents. Where was death? Basements, crawl spaces, freezers? Flogged by the sulfuric breeze, the masked locals avoided small talk and cabbage.

 This tiny locale, Hadenframe, made it on one map when a serial killer and rapist of prominent repute, claimed to have buried over fifty bodies through the smitten landscape where he had also killed his mother. Lauded with three rotted teeth and a mouth full of lies, anyone who met the man doubled back from the stench and audacity.

Texans took a liking to him. He resolved to share all his knowledge with all of the sheriffs in all of the counties. They lined up to meet him in Lubbock. A strawberry milkshake was his reward for every murder he could solve. He smoked thousands of cigarettes as they drove him off highways and under bridges to locations around the country where mutilated bodies of women had been found.

He was on television. Everything was recorded. They only put him in handcuffs when he had to go to court. The county jail was home until the number of his alleged victims approached 400 and then he was electrocuted.

But what of Hadenframe? Can anyone survive that kind of notoriety and vaporous decay? Strange, no matter how much digging in landfills and destruction of houses not one human bone was discovered. Only the resurrected ghostly socket of hissing gingivitis with the sickly haze of strawberry hovering above it.

CRIMINal

My mouth belonged to me.
"Your head is flat as a tape worm."
We waited in line to get measured.
Anything over six inches was condemned as perverse.
Girls lived for high hair.
She said, "Fuck your mother."
"My mother's dead."
She gestured the sign of the cross over her chest and kissed her fingers.
"Catholic freak."

Got roughed up later by her boyfriend. I was a tragedy rotting through schools. Dad, lame in consonants and vowels, expected me to pick up the slack when we moved to a new town. In this place, body hair was a main concern. Dad shaved his moustache in the '70's and I never grew leg hair. We were a colorless vein of Irish transparency. His strawberry hair was mute against the bitter clouds. My head was plastered yellow–limp to the shoulders wisped so thin it scarcely dabbled with a breeze.

Dad spent a week looking for legitimate jobs. I knew that wasn't going to pan out. A girl named Rosella took me on as a possibility. "I like the way your mouth moves," she said. "You say shit to anyone." She had nine kids in her family and most of them "are talkers." Handed her a cigarette the first day and she liked that too.

"Been smoking since I was six," I said. "Used to smoke the butts my dad left in the ashtrays."

"Gross," she said.

"Dad says I have the lungs of an iron-worker."

"Who says stuff like that? What are you, criminals?"

"Maybe," I said, fingering the knife in my pocket.

Acting tough was the only way to make it in the new schools. If you're quiet, you're blindsided. Wanted to know when I was getting attacked and how badly it was going to hurt. Rosella worked on my hair. Lined up products. The bathroom was a beauty salon.

"Can't go out looking like a greaseball," she said. I didn't go anywhere. After school, I went to the public library. I was thirteen. We still lived in the back of Dad's van at Walmart parking lot.

"You're really taking to this place. Look at that hair," Dad said.

Rosella had layered it like one of those soft serve ice cream machines that swirled around and around, but she used gluey paste to hold it up and sprayed more cement-like stuff to cotton candy it higher and higher with each once over. It added a new crop of growth to the top of my head.

"Finally got a job," Dad said. "A little art store in town. Make phone calls all day. Sell toner for word processors. Not exciting, but I'll make some cash so we can rent a place." His head was gutted against his neck. He couldn't even hold it up. I already knew where it was going. Mom was found at the bottom of three flights of stairs off the back porch less than three months ago. Dad never hugged me so much until the cameras.

"We're partners, babe," he kept saying. He was running out of steam. Up for three days. "Yes, Dad." The stench of plastic and hair burned off of his being. Meth. I waited until he passed out in the van. Nabbed his Marlboros and a few dollars out of his pants pocket.

Sat outside on the curb and smoked one after another. My hair, a sculpture in wind, propped itself passive. At some point, a pair of boys around my age walked past. "You could catch a disease from that slut," one said as they laughed.

I grabbed a handful of gravel and took aim. A few landed on the backs of their sweaty necks. They yelled "bitch", then started running back at me. Nothing to lose except time. I stood up, pulled out my switchblade and waited.

She Could Not Offer Herself Up

Violence mutes the odd ghost bones who splay out from family flesh around the dining room table. Every room bloats with a fragrance slick with bruises. The lukewarm simmer of jammed words boil into a bloodied brew accenting tufts of hair and skin and it's only Tuesday. Slant of night chews up whatever light leers through the windows. Dad tumbles out of his briefs into our rooms. It's a deranged pop of another pill, the crush of a derailed penny. Any dictator takes out his bridge of teeth before bed.

The woman he calls wife is not immune to the evening escapades. She lies on the left side of the mattress while her coffin weighs out a single focus: *What's the most efficient way to kill oneself?* Nothing in the house can hold her steady. Medications only vegetate. No help for crying here. The stench is nothing but rage. Defeat has never spun globes.

Sky is loose above the house with the swollen dredge of destitute. Pristine yellow and tawny trim make absent the crumble of interior. No one wakes to memory. Only dreams with stomach aches or fevers consecrate the crest of another day.

The wife backs her station wagon out drunk and rising from the cracks. A bridge sits and waits. Time is no longer a confrontation. A flask filled with fucking everything. Nobody says grace at her table. It is their killing fields. She buckles the kids in. They have a ways to go.

LiTTERiNg CONflICT

A magazine article kidnaps me while on the toilet. The crying husband's rheumy eyes showcase his guilt, but it takes them a year or so to figure that out. They'll drag out the conflict, until one day, action, resolution and that guy with the haircut of a five-year-old will lose the dimples and his latest wife.

If the planet is so absurd then why shouldn't we mimic it. Conflict cows inside the stomach. A man comes close. I hold a bag of groceries and wear head phones on the way home at dusk. The man moves closer every time I look behind. My pace picks up and when I turn his arms are over my head. 'Fuck no,' and my bag wallops the guy's face. I scream 'fire'. He runs. A soup can rolls under my heel and knocks me back on the cement. It is my body, the torn paper bag, bread, milk, cans, and a cracked bottle of wine. Aren't people supposed to run out of buildings when they hear 'fire'? Well, that is just one agonizing moment of many. Really, if I razor through my thoughts I find more humiliation and botched transgressions in the mundane than I do in the extraordinary.

Everything is irregular and dusty when I get home from a writing workshop; especially books. A distortion of colors and shapes weep along bookshelves all over the living room like so many eyes wondering what I won't do with a day. Probably read. Minutes spread a long pulsating hangover.

There is a calendar in every room, but no sense of keeping track. A day is a day is a day is. Coffee slugs through me. I understand beverages. Themes search like a rolodex for death. Life. Love. Hate. Time. Speedball. Caffeine wracks through my system until there's no choice but to expel something.

Guilt throws books on the bed. One opens. Drops. Then another. Two cats fight, race up and down stairs. The clock keeps watch. Rains and gets colder. More books roost in this place unread than read. A film of soot over some keeps me from further examination. What the hell did the writer say? Conflict, action, and resolution in each scene. A story must parade in this order across a well-eaten page. Blood on the paper is a bad joke. One of the stories I gave back to a writer in the workshop had brown stains on it that plastered a more digressive or putrid thought in mind. I unpack clothes and stuff them in the washer. The clock still waits when I return. If only I could drink. It is just after noon. Another cuticle rolls around my tongue.

Remember the masterpieces studied. Sentences stack neatly. Coins roll into paper homes. Conflict, action, resolution. Wouldn't it be exquisite if the skies blacken and somber? Wouldn't it be one of those stooped days when weather does the work for the depreciated? I just returned from a week of note-taking I can't decipher and squint-provoking thoughts. Cats are out of water. Kitty litter is lumpy. Clock; ridiculous.

The instructor says, digest material. Burn notes– one of my favorite ways to warm myself. Lay away from writing. Give it a week or so. What if the work roughhouses and comes up with words that thumb through conflicts as if they were assailants? What if nothing comes from this Tuesday? Something appears out of these thin-lipped clouds? If I sink another shot of caffeine and pop that beer I might assemble something that at least scaffolds a dumpster of ideas.

Irritation has nothing better to do than sit on me.

Conflict: My head is a grave full of undetonated mines.

Action: I mistake it for another run to the bathroom.

Resolution: The clock runs laps around sanity. I crack open a beer.

The Pedophile's Test: Mutiny of Disturbance

I hurt my victim.

What does the child know of comfort? Mom hides in the kitchen each night. I shackle my cowgirl in scrubbings brusque and swollen. "Crucified deflowerings," I call them. "You're a bit of a vial buster, you pint of soot and slather. The dirty is done. Let me wipe up your vicious parts till they whimper." She is five years old.

The victim actually wanted sex.

She turns over like a goddamn breeze. Daylight presses through the window. Quick. Do it when my son mows the lawn. Gentle fingers permeate. Snail her slowly. I jack off leaning in. At some point high heels slaughter the wooden steps moving up toward us from the first floor. The pull back is fit as a peck on the cheek. I flip her. A knock at the door. "Honey?" The knob clicks. Mom peers in. "You two are damn precious," Mom laughs. Snaps a photo. I smile. "Get out of here," yell and kiss the air.

In reality, I was only educating my victim.

Make sure the kid has her own room. When Mom's asleep I hedge in. "Don't be scared. Home is love, babe. Nasty boys slap you upside alleys and leer after it's done. No reason to humiliate yourself. Math is calculation, practice, and memorizing formulas. Let your hands roam, little madam. Learn me. Cover the map with your family questions."

I masturbate to fantasies of my victim.
Buy a nice scarf from the dime store. Choose by color I sniff off each kid. No cotton candy pink for girls. Some roar with winds can slice whatever boy out of anyone. Coil her neck and saturate the cum. A tie rack in the basement separates the stench. Close my eyes and a mist shivers rising tremors. Cleanest memory I ever have. Waterfalls. Expand with each child lingering over me. I remember you. I remember every little piece of you.

Honestly, I can say I cried for my victim.
Blood frightens me. Thick and sore. The kid is a goddamn river of hurt. Holding her insides in. Face splotched as the blood clots, dark and raw. So tiny. I try to unfill her. Keep it unsealed and wet with me. Not her. Baby lotion in the bassinet. Pink creases unspoiled as a baby rabbit. She wanders my face with her rips. What have I done?

It wasn't my fault.
There are always two. One navigates roads. The other embraces them. I smack her friend away from the van. Cheeks scrabble the baby rant flushing reds and whites like puzzle pieces across her face. "Get out, kid." The door slams shut. We move. Nothing but side roads. Those passive shaky lines lending a hand to nowhere on the map. The kid has

a cherubic face with no extra chins or strange caves. Who wouldn't find beauty in that? The kid huddles into herself and cries.

"It's okay. It's okay," I say. This sniffling cesspit of agony is dragging me into the muck of childhood. "Here kid, drink this." Her lips keep shuddering as her mouth clamps shut. "Who's the adult here?" I ask. We pull off the road. I clutch her gurgling jaw. "Suck it in," I say… that's it, princess. Whiskey kisses us." At some point her eyelids wane. I stare into the marble skin and lips blood-soak pump with 'fuck me.'

ENDURANCE

In service to gesticulating men she dissociates from the crush of her husband's crumbs, one blue blade of sky. Cold blots stem her extremities that scuttle the corridors of routine. She tests the stupor of her smile, fifteen years of placating the low tide of rooms, the clutch of barbed newspapers, the stench of regulars anticipating a lover, each with the silent shriek of special. "Good morning, Keith. A double espresso and blueberry scone," flutter through his ache.

Bodies tremor when her vast stretch of 'I parade you' wraps around an ego like an overwrought bouquet. "Scott: two shots vanilla, iced latte, breakfast burrito." Scott suspends within her pillow of feathers, forgets he is married and hates his job. He is all manner of things with her. No one dismisses him here.

Every day orbit of humans reek the same moist weight of disclosure. She is the vacancy they fill with their secrets. "Skim milk for Bob," "Chai for Larry," "Cappuccino for Bret with egg/ham sandwich." Three homeless customers sleep, read all day. She feeds. Coffee unlimited.

*   *   *   *

No one wonders about her cracks. The doors lock. The sky a flat sheet over her head. She is narcotized by night combed in the same direction. Go home. Husband is out. Power process of her thoughts begin. Keys on the counter. Is this the only way to raise your flag? Post-it notes are scripted with messages for the EMT's, friends, family. Nothing intoxicates a frenzy. She is thoughtful and methodical.

Helium. Plastic bag with elastic. Pipe from gas container into bag. Breathe out. One hour at the most. Deep breaths.

Shelter Me, Dark Artery

Bungle escape, batter of luggage wheels clack over cement, curse intention and vacancy. Pockmarks troll skin, suck blood out of scabs older than family. Shudder of hot and cold smother the weight of air she can't get enough of. Nothing but pain winces ahead of her. No money, no home, no smokes, no time. Dying has come closer to her than this. Make the streets cushion people with baggies, tinfoil, lighters.

Oxycontin shaves on to tinfoil like a shot and a prayer. Sport me a light, honey. Slide right across silver spoons elixirs of gold. Hold tight. Keep the door shut on the lungs long.
Nice pull. No one leaks their genitals in her face this time. Can't recall a gift this large without stealing.

Rehab is sleep storms and war deeper inside. Scratch at old creeps.

Man chokes, she begs.
Man calls men. Her ass: revolver entrance.
Man sharpens a hatchet. Cuts off her fuck finger. Pay up.
Man landmines through her brain. She runs a soup kitchen of blow-jobs.

Intervention day: 2 kids, mom, dad, grandmother, some lady full of back talk.

A cackle of voices spread out:
"See her on the streets. Don't tell anyone she's my mom."
"Took all my jewelry, when she had a key."
"Can't she get a fucking pair of dentures?"
"Look at her."
"Cops used to send her back to us."
"Dead before the room unnerves her."

She finds some cardboard.
High sky meek with whispering clouds.
Remote world unwraps.
Soon days will be severed.

Family Recipe

Stuff the gluten in potatoes, suicide-up with Aunt Mary. Can you smell the garlic of mute? Slits her veins in a kitchen-less room with a block top counter. A stampede of kids and husband, full as a field mouse gorge through TV dinners. Green peppers flatter meatballs, sweet sweat of Mom's psychosis. Neighbors perpetrate paprika of paranoia. Brown in a lampless room, voices pierce, mix, spit out bites of contention. Ravioli is cockful of Crisco, can't suck sauce under 350 degrees. Baby veal thighs bleed tender to touch, tremor of bourbon licks their flanks. The burn hurls through cigarette smoke after carcass.

All voices are anorexic.

Too Much Outside Coming In

"You know, we've all got something. Finally forced myself out of bed after the rape, thought I could salvage other girls. Victim's advocate. No pay and I was glad for it. They gave me a beeper and sent me out walking the cage of city at night. Dogs gave a heads-up. They were warnings; not background sound. I didn't hear them, at first, and got dragged into an alley right outside the hospital with the victim I was supposed to reassure waiting inside. I mean what is that?"

Lisa, a white girl with dreadlocks and a face splotched with need, was triggered by this frayed character who didn't chit-chat. Whoever named her Cookie must have despised her. Lisa felt compelled to spew. "I slept a good long time between retail and food service jobs. What you got littering your landscape? Every girl has something."

The sky was a wrecked blather of gray and blue.

Cookie pushed herself up and sat there. "Yeah," she nodded. "We're some kind of dolls they spit into the world to be fucked. Things happened to me. Yeah, they did."

Cookie sat and listened to the pit bull finish his meal. It was barely mid-morning. She was already tired and ready to quit this job too. Everything smelled of prisons and blood.

The Space We Occupy

I walk home. The sun grinds. How come it smells like my rank retainer?

I sweat between veins of fat-dripping sky. Prying eyes limit each step as if stoned under enormous weights. Every muscle distracts from its neighbor. I don't know how to maneuver this body, deranged and stiff. Ten days and nine nights withering back to the man with no face who thrashes holding his semi-erect penis inside me, the burn full of knife.

The man wears a pillowcase over his head. He whispers "shut-up" softly as if shushing a kid to sleep. His stink, of decay and cigarettes. Spreads himself in a battleground. Loose skin sticks to my flesh. An open window no longer illuminates the gaze of an indifferent view.

I want to stride like I used to. Bounce past sirens, stumble over sewer grills, text my boyfriend. But none of the screeching peacocks in the city around me know how easy it is to die inside.

Snapshot

Carnal colors infiltrate a cloud in silence within a city no more yellow than before. A man clutches a girl's twisting body. Her tiny face harbors an invincible battalion that smacks of war. She is thrown into a van. The locked door is a weapon.

The tall man puts on loud music and drives. There are smudged lacey window drapes along the back of the van. She slits one open. The windows are painted black. The man is laughing. He's watching her in the rearview mirror. She won't remember the color of his eyes.

A video of a herd of buffalo stop traffic for miles in a town with mountains. She used to watch it over and over. All those cars stuck and the passengers stand outside to capture the event on their phones. Hope drags its ugly head when her dog gets hit by a neighbor's car a week later and dies.

The man drives through a McDonalds and gets a Happy Meal and three orders of fries. "Here, Princess," he says. "What's your favorite food?" he asks. "If I had to have a last meal it would be a gallon of fries."

The mountains love animals. She wants a monkey, a llama, and at least four goats. The suburbs pretend space for everyone with fat lawns and attics, but she is confined to a tiny room next to her parents. The dents in the plaster get bigger every time her mom and dad scream.

How did this man find out she wants to run away? Her older brother already moved out. He sends her postcards, even though she dreams he is still sleeping in the attic.

Dear Sister,
Stay in your room as much as possible. Mark off the years. You have to get through two years of grade school, and four years of high school. Everything is street and full of itself and wants to destroy. Close your blinds.

It is all trees and no sky. Bird squawks blast through the dead wood. The man clutches her by the waist as their shoes crunch deeper into the forest. She knows an endless line of girls has stepped here before her. It's all news. How simple it is to disappear.

HUMiliaTioN iN iNSTallMeNTS

Older sister tells me not to go out on a Friday night because
there are predators on the streets, gets picked up by a
boyfriend who smacks her every time they're together. She
smacks back, but he's an ex-Marine and clocks her face
more than she does his.

Everyone adores the guy in high school. He broods the
demeanor of an unreachable assurance everybody yearns.
The confidence, the chiseled face, smirk looks like he's in
on a private joke. Steel-toe boots, straight-leg jeans, and the
badass bomber jacket the pack wears. He is a Marine so god
knows how old he really is. He calls Dad, Sir, and shakes his
hand. Older sister narrows her eyes. Dad's relief is visible.
She's in the boyfriend's care and not Dad's. She rips patches
of Dad's hair off his scalp when they go head to head.

I'm not like older sister. Reciprocating hasn't been my
agenda. My cheek planks against Dad's palm more than a
few times. My boyfriends are chronically shy like me. We
converse in stilted movements.

Imagine when the Marine is a kid. Eyes soft as rotten melons.
Hate creates violence and frustration, and the will to live as
strong as his Dad's fist. A hierarchy to beatings and torture
follow a pattern. Dad beats Mom. Dad beats kid. Kid tortures

dog and various animals in the neighborhood. Kid tortures younger kids. Kid grows taller and stronger than Dad. Kid beats Dad. Kid gets kicked out of the house.

Kid sleeps in his car, stays overnight on weekends for a year in different friends' houses and streets. Gets a job as a janitor at the high school. By sixteen he is accepted by the Marines. I can't guess how many years he spends as a soldier. Up until this point, these are all journal entries of what the Marine does and how he grows up.

Sister doesn't ask. I prod her for information. She ignores me. But, you see, it all grows dim and forests. The Marine comes back and goes to high school with us. He smokes pot and drinks beer. His back is straight up, obedient.

Sister and him fight, have sex. One night I am the last girl, besides Sister, in the park with about ten older guys. I act as though Sister, the Marine, and I are a trio when they've long forgotten me. I sit on the bumper of the station wagon drinking a beer when the car starts to rock up and down. Moans crescendo from inside. My face turns purple and my body shakes. The guys snicker as they watch me. I want to dismember my sister. Time is lewd and gives no reprieve. Every humiliating moment I've lived clasps hands and circles around me as I bounce up and down with the car. The windows steam up. I can't even write in my journal for weeks. I'm sick with cringing.

Sister and the Marine have the fight of all fights when she smacks him a final time.

"You want it straight? Well, guess what? I'm not."

The Marine screams, "Queer. Fucking queer," over and over. Sister runs inside.

Flowers are delivered to the house. He parks outside our house for weeks. Whenever she goes out she leaves by the back door. Sometime after that a magazine in a brown paper wrapper appears with Sister's name on it.

No one gets magazines in our family. Mom is a librarian and doesn't believe in what she calls 'journalistic jackasses'. Sister opens the wrapper. A girl in half a bikini with huge boobs she hugs and *Playboy* in huge letters spreads across the front.

"Fucker," Sister says and runs upstairs crying.

I pick up the magazine and quietly take it to my room.

PaNTOUM: CRiMe SCeNe

You remember the forms assault took on
when you were fucked. The cold slither
of wet slapping between your legs.
The stench of rubber mixed with humiliation.

When you were fucked. The cold slither
A white rubber hose hanging from the hot-water bottle
The stench of rubber mixed with humiliation.
 You count how many flower petals on each cobalt tile

A white rubber hose hanging from the hot-water bottle
remember how many species are the color of blood.
You count how many flower petals on each cobalt tile
You are naked in a bathroom with your dad.

Remember how many species are the color of blood
You are undone piece by piece
You are naked in a bathroom with your dad.
You are letting him stick things up you.

You are undone piece by piece
An echo is in this room
You are letting him stick things up you.
He knows this is a crime scene.

You are letting him stick things up you.
You are letting him undo you piece by piece
 because you have never believed in the whole of you.
An echo in this room. He is yelling.

He knows this is a crime scene
You are the patient. Not the mangled silence
 that gargles around this Wednesday afternoon.

One bathroom in the house. Seven people squirm
and creak through the labyrinth of unlocked doors.
Later, you will study the blood in your stools.
An echo in this room. He is yelling.

Take Back The Streets

"Never finish everything on your plate. What are we, paupers?" Grandma caws after each meal.

The family heirloom is choking on the leftovers of its own absence. We rot from misuse and empty space.

Every day I urge my belittling; smaller my body. I angulate into a bent-up receptacle like the last battered section of toothpaste. My psyche buries itself for a time in the landscape of white powder, a mirror and a blade. How cavernous my riotous sinkhole of person shores up to display its nerves. I walk in on a party of strangers. Lines of coke are divvied out for ten people on a glass table. They smile at me as a large man slices out another line. "You," he says. A silent grenade detonates out of the glitter landmine of me. I snort, shoot, rake every last shimmer of dust on that table. Breaking for the door the room is war bleeding armies spitting seed in my wake, teeming multitudes of roaring yesterdays are trampling over each other to skeleton me, and I'm running, I'm running as though a bony hand isn't throttling my throat.

I run. I run every day. I run until the veins in my legs are confrontational. Sideways speaks to strangers and tells them what to do. Air wraps around me and holds me prey. A man with a stomach packed with malignancy grabs at the movement of me. He catches depletion and takes it by the wrist. Slips a knot through it and pulls its cage to his car. My loose hair slides easily through the window. He rapes me.

Years whisk in and out behind alleys. There is weather and numerous facts we cannot comprehend. Steven Hawkings dies. His books are displayed and bought, but incomprehensible as fat. I have mutated into an exhibit. I wear buildings beneath my skin. Sideways is a full parking lot with a security guard. I eat through seasons. Grandmother dies of lack. Mom dies of certitude. A runt does not thrive. A runt lives beneath sick winds and bodies. I barrel through aisles after midnight jacking up on ice cream sandwiches, cookies, and cheesecake. One white powder has turned itself off for another. A man is glinting towards me. He smiles and tries to rip the streets out from under me. Tonight I watch retribution shudder like a slice of panic.

I shift my weight through a city that thrusts back revulsion every handful of blocks. Men choke the sidewalks forging my girth to battle. Malleable pouches of skin get bumps and grinds from crass bodies, but the waves ripple and slosh right over anything that might bite. There's more space in the sky tonight. Swollen with revelry, my steps champion the cement.

No Time To Look Back

As soon as you've stepped inside, you're bolted in. Rotted stories bristle and battle each other in a grudge, closing into groaning flesh. Just open the door while moving. Trees and cornfields careen as fast as your mind. A casual swipe of a moment and clouds shake heads in only one direction. The cord, the handcuffs, a whole maintenance man's box of tools. Look deeply at the crusty creases of stubble and eyes as demented as yours must be. Talk. Say what? Words beg to be laughed at. Cry? Nothing but one tic that creeps through your left eye. It seems there is no hero in this van. Nothingness bares itself. Worthless streets dumb as his mouth blink past you.

That girl who was blindfolded and lifted it enough so she could route it to memory. The girl who heard planes overhead and they found her kidnapper lived by the airport. The girl who talked a man into tears, telling him she was dying of AIDS. Go ahead, kill her.

You have lost the ability to care. Let him drudge you with his wicked idiocy. Let his DNA drip into your orifices. Someone will file them away in plastic bags. You've seen the shows. Where would you be if you weren't here? Maybe gym class. In those blue bloomers. Fucking focus.

He's far enough away from here not to know where there will become. All of it seems to wane away. The white van passes naked in and out of landscapes without a game plan. It's a seedy ghost that vacates anyone's vision. When it comes to a shuddering halt, there is no betrayal.

There are the trees crowded together, weary with anticipation. Beyond them as many paths that end somewhere. As many crunching leaves as he will need.

The Rumble of the Vicious

The dick waits. Girl goes online. White van is surfing the web now. One Snapchat of girl rendering infinity her childlike tits. In Europe beaches are topless. His right hand is travel. School is encased with ghosts. Bumped, pushed through, plowed past. Competition is a fucking mighty rock. Heads pause in disappointment when shy isn't exploited. Not yet. Drowns her with adjectives. A smile wears her in a manic pulse. Weapons face screens with their own groping reflections. A suburb within suburbs of webcams bleed into one another. The age of boy and girl is a bruise of syncopation. He leers over her edges at school.

She needs no forest. She needs no bathroom stall. Her bedroom spins in a polaroid orbit. He caresses his streaks of stubble. "Flash me," he types. "You're a goddamn star." She leans back and thrusts her hips into the voice. The audience is inside her. She is greasy with crotch and writhing fame. "Flash me," he whispers. "You are my flame."

Mom is comatose downstairs. The laugh track pushes wind into her lungs. Fingers curl around the remote. She stares at the ceiling. Listens for her daughter. Music breathes through the closed door. The kid is fourteen and plump with conspiracy. "Nothing," Mom repeats over and over. She cups an empty wine glass, wonders if she can pour another without the kid noticing.

The girl has practiced the click of her bra, powerful as any fist of anonymity. The screen studies her. No one has ever looked so deeply. Fourteen-years old. Radiance is the night mute with golden whispers. "Flash. Flash. Flash," he sprawls his lust through the spreadeagle room. The curve of her rice paper shoulder, the tiny, satin rose smitten in between breasts. She curls herself around, holding her lower back. Her hips ache. Thick with a thousand eyes waiting for the final act.

His camera readies to click the stills. Not going to work some lowlife pizza place. This is his enterprise. Same as always. Modulate the voice, hone in, vibrate against her limpid days. "You're choking my world, babe. I have to have you. No one can do what you do."

Each word tongues back on her. Bent in toward breath she cannot hear, she unclasps the bra. Arching her being, she quakes in the swelter of blunt devotion.

*　*　*　*

He knows how it works. The best still of her face with breasts is sent to backpage.com so the pedos can have her first. The pay is as good as the suits. Then she's put up on Facebook.

Her name is corner enough to saturate the school. Tagging alerts persecute her narrative. Beige streets that spiral through the slaughter of a girl's dare to be, she is hunted. Words spill bullet for bullet while whispers tangle the air around her. She is alone.

*   *   *   *

She transfers to another school. His breath follows her. Mom hears about it the morning after she takes a bottle of Advil. The boy already has the promise of another's unscathed flesh.

Anyone Can Guess

Sit in a chair, stare at another uplifted eyebrow and wonder what you can add. I'd smack you if you said I am still alive and mapping through 35 more years of therapy. I straggle down this 'I'm sorry' path planking the same nightmares trying to find a goddamn unplugged toilet with a stall door. This psychiatrist has family junkyard tomes. The one before fusses with the meds. Does anyone know childhood suffocates as quickly as a bad check? Let's talk about pancreatic cancer, younger than us, strapped in a car seat stringing its light to the veins. It all secretes hollow history next to that night littering home from a bar when it spirals bloody.

Three more blocks. I say *I won't* when metal grazes my neck. The siren pelts over miles of a city in transit. I am coiled on the grimace of a gun. *'Kill you, bitch,'* is the desperate fabric. Over and over it stinks of cowardice. Could it be? My suicide pact unbeds itself.

Pay Attention

The girl becomes revenge in this geography where only pain exists. Blather, correct, falsify a train track, the corner of a curb, the leg of a highway. Who says something holds up? Divide in order to exist. Lurk eager. Lurk desperate. Why the long coat? Her nod bounces off the bone.

He swells like a mouth full of Bible. Fester any spare change? Time trades his strange for sweat. Go fathom all she can't muster. Pick, chop, cut the itch away. Swallow her up while she strains fat as the footpath to her insides. A very fine coven his scramble of tics.

Quiet rots riot between them. Nothing idle beneath the burl of blanket pooling her body. The beat of each other listens to itself. Each pothole on the journey withers the known of them.

Hiss of the Desolate Street

Squandered tomorrows stunt into rotted yesterdays. Her head swills with the stink of man tongue still in the teeth, spray of body grit. Nothing carries on without the lick of droning confusion. She has been with four, five, six men tonight. This will be the last. He flicks out sharpened tools, tiny jaws of dental instruments from a backpack. Not to be forgotten.

Welcome to the vacancy of her haunches. She is tied, gnaws at plastic sky. The man carves rations of her, cookie-cutter, screaming tumor scourged with Brillo pads, flesh burn steeps in fury, gorges eyes gaze from her chest, magazine holes doom this woman into what he lacks.

He snaps photographs, studies the dark brew of his precision. She encompasses the van like a prison cell. The sharp lines of streets and alleys risk revealing his ravenous convulsions. It is time to clear the evidence before there is no outlet.

The woman decays, merges with a bounty of black garbage bags in a dumpster before the air pulsates with the swell of her steaming blood.

MaRRiage DOeSN'T TURN a CORNeR

Dad roams for hitchhikers
Mom roams for fizzy boxed booze
Dad rants aggressive shaving
Mom rants he is terminally erect

Dad mists after a Swedish film seduces him
Mom mists after Dad begs to asphyxiate
Dad pockets a fistful of Mom's Valium
Mom pockets Dad's red, white, and blue speedos

Mom calls them underpants
Dad calls them panties
Mom wakes up mornings a swollen ingenue
Dad wakes up mornings a post-traumatic whore

Mom slaps naked Dad reciting Rilke's letters
Dad slaps naked Mom butt-scooting over carpet like the
dog
Mom grinds five-inch-stilettos slightly above Dad's jugular
Dad grinds Earth shoes and Transcendental Meditation
back into closets.

Mom loses eyesight.
Dad loses days and nights.

Grope, they do. One rot-iron day vows are exchanged
again.

Will trains stop or continue?

Will saucepans gurgle?

Dad stands at the edge of her bed.

It is clearly marked 'hot springs.'

He strips.

Mom holds her breath.

HiS GeSTUReS MaY Be UNReMaRKable

The jowls of a man of knowledge are weighed down by a hefty lifetime of facts. He is a man of damp bitterness and answers. The verge of too much thought can wear him down to his bed midday. But don't expect him to lie still for more than twenty minutes. There is nothing illusive about his pursuits. Every day the papers fill their obligation to rise. His fingers keep a steady tempo of typing. A habit of licking the underside of his teeth keep time with the clicking.

Every once in a while he looks out his window. A bird sometimes sits on his tree limb. He feels something lift in his heart region. If a storm is lurking, he is cocooned inside and the edges of the pages are softer and his words become almost poetic. A tremendous peace envelops him when he has nowhere to go and no one to see. The words and sentences unroll themselves. The computer loves him. It whispers thoughts into his fingertips that trouble the page. And slowly images start to imprint themselves in his mind and once they have been deadlocked on the screen, they manifest into his archival jowls.

He cradles bodies inside there too. The holidays always bring on a holiday high and time with relatives. His great-aunt Peppy was dying in the backroom of his mother's house for over a year. She was sick with discomfort and talked to anyone who would listen about making an end to it, if only. One night he put on the Dylan Thomas Christmas album and stirred some granules of arsenic and drops of morphine into her straw-full of liquid. She was so close to dying that the hospice nurse wrote 'Failure to Thrive' on the death certificate. That led him to her best friend, Berta, who was going blind and was almost deaf. Her family had just put her in a home. They didn't live in the same city, so she had few visitors. When Peppy died, Berta was heartbroken. That crushed the man of knowledge. He read some of his stories to her and books, as well. The lonely were a fattening crowd. He saw them on the streets everywhere. They showed up in his work. Tears blathered down his cheeks when he was writing. He loved the sick and the dying. They spoke truths and he listened. Most of the world cranked itself up with noise. They demanded sing-a-longs and pig roasts and all kinds of barbaric meanderings.

His words lessened themselves. At some point, he could only read aphorisms. Anything longer and he found ragged hounding dialogue with two leeches, one trying to suck the other dry.

After Berta died, he volunteered for hospice. He was taking a class on herbs and what their attributes are and learned quickly. He found his community. He excluded the rest of the world each night when he locked his shutters.

But he let the feverish reality rule his computer. He thought of all the people who had died. And then an aphorism would arise from the cremations and memorials he'd attended.

"Humans are absurd. We live not for our daily bread, but for our schedules. Whenever we react to the suffering of the sum total of a life and toast it, we are astonished by the smoking dried crust of audacity that fogs our doom."

Then the weight of all of the timid shrouds.

Loose on the Bones

In her mouth like a man let this cage collapse. Shave, modulate at midnight. Again and again these predators strike. Bludgeon the soot of young girls. As they age and blur, uteruses become dumpster trash. Held together by something torn apart, animalesque. Squawks rasp from toothless trends. Crotchrot is a phenomenon. Strangers encroach, press into her space until decay. Scale fences. Bite off telephones with whispers of 'kill,' 'I see you,' 'don't forget me.' Tighten to refuse their owling eyes. Her hands unravel for the lives she used to sweat. No longer. Bed, this ancient of night, smother and repeat. Count her gone. Plunge into estrange. Vagrancy swallows behind tightened blinds. He watches. He waits.

Impaled Flight

There was the hum of stragglers, the musky odor of trash filled the air when his arm wrapped me. Kept me stranded among the so-called living. A thousand fists. Once, I struggled. Dark halls to motel rooms. I lied and stumbled into the truth. Don't count on a hollow man dropping. Do not think to climb me, mister. Heard him lap at the wound. Sharp and unsung. Rough unbridled head I shook. Am I thawed from history? Locusts and fascists. Barren generations sucked the guns. Prevented my reflection from escape. Never unclenched the cramp of me. Left me counterfeit and divided.

POLYPS

Lower frequencies speak under eyelids. It's a desolate journey of the colon's weave of the wheel. Count backwards from three and time is neither skim nor splash. No doubt the subterfuge discovers itself in the passage. Light dims. The hunt is for mushrooms.

Assault on quantity of clutter. Mishmash of odor, dust, mold, or other types of structural damage. Hoarding extends beyond overstuffed homes. Health risks can damage families. Affect surrounding neighborhoods. Treating it requires more than boxes of trash bags.

People acquire things. If they no longer cook meals, can't live safely at home, threaten others, that's where it reeks of childhood.

Lie in a fetal position. Left side. Veins hem in like plucked eyebrows. Nurse pokes haggard digs, says if I drank the entire gallon of liquid laxative the vein would manifest as plump as a gorged vagina. An image lingers of: my face after mosquito bites, balloons, and yeast infections.

An intense emotional attachment to objects that others see as trivial—or even trash. They'd feel a sense of major loss if they had to throw this stuff away.

Leave part of myself stranded on the other side. I find a pornographic magazine in the garage under tires, oil cans, unknown paintings on cardboard. I take it to my room. Black and white, old, in a language I can't decipher. But the photos? A sense that many items have an intrinsic value, like others might see in artwork or driftwood.

Collecting wood for a fire. Found a precious stalk of wood with arms and an erect penis. Won't burn him.

The assumption that an item might be useful someday, which compels them to save far more than "the drawer of hinges, thumbtacks, string, and rubber bands" that many of us keep. An unfinished outhouse that looks on as the shit refuses to exit. Forget the hurry to get somewhere.

It's Not Every Day...

Biking pants tightened like a wrench around the serial killer's waist ten years ago, even five. His gut, pompous and center-stage, had pregnated a brute with age. He had to wear sweatpants from here on out. Jump a fence now and the fence would win. Twenty years of a night job teemed with bodies, whipped, bled, shot and raped. The stench of guttural fluids coursed through his nostrils that no shower dispelled. His wife and kids frayed from emitting peacock sirens cranked up on televisions molesting streets.

Sullen couples crested murder in their minds, images of pockmarked screens ripped open sloppy as unwrapped presents. Creaks, windows shuddered, stairs struck, shapes assumed. Houses took intruders in as if tossing crumbs to a pigeon. The neighborhood no longer ran itself.

The serial killer used the gate instead of the fence. He crouched in the backyard. A family was eating dinner through this particular illuminated room. He had turned channels on these local stations for decades. Parents had sex, teenagers had sex, kids took baths, parents took showers, walked around naked, fought, beat their kids, drank vodka out of gallon jugs, smoked pot, snorted cocaine, did it all as though no one could see them. He used to stand for hours and experience their bullshit first-hand.

The urge was still there. The killer had his mask, gloves, gun, rope, tape, and knives. He also had sciatica which raged up his left leg when he stood too long. Tonight it was unsparing and raw. And, damn it, his wife was cooking lasagna.

VaST KNOT OF MiSCellaNeouS LiVeS

Today is pleasurably mute, infused with the stillness of the manswarm. There pervades a comforting lack of voices on a late Sunday afternoon. That point outside when darkness clings to the last strain of light before succumbing to its inevitable aloneness. Bracing itself for that shudder of solitude. Its lonely plight without fail. The waning hours paint themselves more dismally on this day when streets call out to take refuge in their blank, silent embrace. Maybe a chorus of a million mute cries bank off the muddy puddles, endless rain taps against the panes that stare out with a frightened eye and wonder what it is they must do.

Numberless cold plates sit on tabletops, scatter remains of potatoes, carrots. Endless hands hold forks in bleary kitchens as eyes stare out of icebox windows into other darkened windows. Row after row, street after street, single lit rooms trail one another until each blurs into the next, yet somehow exist apart.

A travesty of foggy dreams splay out into the damp atmosphere, multiply through the soot-ridden avenues. Anyone dares to walk these sidewalks spirals into cacklings of empty hope. Pedestrians glut with aches of fixations–an invisible collusion links the melancholy plight like holding hands with the ruinous multitude, as though one's own weight wasn't enough.

Rain, winds rise like sounds of Mahler. The winding trances of woodwinds. Battling wail of flutes. Lurk of the brass surrounds.
The sinking doom of another day imprisons us with its rattling monotony; its migraine pace. The conspiratorial rasp of the clock snickers and the numb tread of men loop the same track with impunity.

I sit in my kitchen, fork dangling in my fingers. I look out into the dim light of a kitchen with another hunched figure who leans over his plate, who stares out a window at yet another figure. We watch for the creep of hours like the face of another life. Not long before strangers batter into our lives again.

Who WaS IT?

Mother died today. Slaughtered like memory. Buried cells past. Eyes a tragedy. Unhinge her skull. Imagine her alive. Shattered window shards. Quaff, questioned, qualm. Private hospital rooms. Electric shock therapy. Dad signed papers. Dry, muted tongues. Jeerful, hideous husband. Sex addict status. Xenophobic Irish neighborhood. Catholic sheep sheared. Six total births. One child stillborn.

Mom's beige sister. Four total births. Lunacy of intrusion. Convulsed, mad chaos. Too much noise. Fragments scattered her. Diffused outside terror. Unkempt choral clocks. Half-baked skies. Nights groped yesterdays. Hands circuited rooms. She was seven. The uncle babysat. Her breath impotent. Uncle groaned thunder. Bleary, overgrown carpet. Mom was nine. That year hissed.

Depression transfixed gestures. Grizzled efforts dissolved. Faces never migrated. Nothing rediscovered dawn. The sisters dissolved. Mom: cancer castaway. Aunt: slit throat. Fetid photograph albums.

Kids rotted indifference. They became addicts. They became thieves. They became Jesuits. Dad's fluttered on. Found vigorous wives. Sparkling, white wine. Yoga begot scourge.

They detested offspring. Cleaned, cleaned, disinfected. Screamed, yelled, eradicated. "Fucking get out."

Kids ambushed exits. They got out.

Make No Mistake;
Foretaste of Loss

Woods pucker and groan. Two kids start the drought. Two more. Then two more. Hysteria creeps deftly through screen doors and open windows. Shut, lock, shut, lock. Tiny towns gnaw through nights. Dark streets sandwich between porch lights.

A conscience makes it tough. First kid is soft corners with braids that smell of weeds, tides of pain with no polish. She's a bumblebee, but wants to be a tree. I snatch her like a houseplant searches for sun, call her Oak. She devours adventurous books from the library. Tells me, "Mister, I've got six brothers and a whole pack of cousins, and you'll never guess. I'm the only girl. Can you even…" I revel in her, until I don't.

Second one staggers through grass, a nest of hair knots and venom. Spits and pummels. I smile and say, "Time to go home, honey," as a lady passes and sighs. "Now, listen to your daddy, little girl," shakes her finger, rolls her eyes and laughs. Just another holiday as this body migrates to the dank layers of pine and dead branches.

I'm a magnet for snarl and dispute. Unmoor in the city. Two go missing from the Bronx. The delicate disaster of overwrought parents keep me in flesh-flutter fruit. No one knows where anyone is anymore. Savage innocence is rampant and terror is well-fed. Let me give you the grave I walk on.

Are we not privy to the whine of zealous ministers who bombast silence in evil service to the theft of our precious, virtuous fuel.

Rusting in a Back Lot

Three abortions and a pack of smokes later, she houses in one of those sheds. Sixteen years old, she rakes through time like a goddamn rolodex. When she is six, no one notices men with tongues flattened against playground fences.

Same number of concrete squares. Sidewalk collapses into sleepy steps home with eyes closed. One grit of a man grinds himself under her heels. Not a kid or parent red lights the girth of Officer Friendly. No one plagues the stranger's plan. Sucks her inside his van. Chokes in her own solitude. Six years old, easy as a candy bar shoplift. Gone.

Everyone goes on about the neighborhood angst. Signs they put up. Parents plead for the kid. Please, they say. Rewards. 5,000, 10,000 and no conviction if you just give her back.

That shit blows in the wind of nothing in less than two weeks. Ten years later? Please. No scars are left. Photos remain. Memories remain. But, a body? No.

Family and friends come together once a year to curl in the leaks of her being. No cops. That is a done deal.

WhEN WiLL MY RaPiST'S CloSET BE ClEaNEd?

"Hysteria comes from the Greek root hystera, meaning 'uterus'. Originally, it was believed that hysteria and hysterical symptoms were caused by a defect in the womb, and thus, only women could become hysterical."

—Shalome Sine

Vivid and startled, blood spits out a song, a sigh, signals a stale rustle of corruption. A pulse rouses itself from the uterus. And those subterranean tubes palpate the last fumes of incessant weather before swirling the rays of dusk down the toilet. I am a girl of fugitive parts. Cut with a straight knife. Glue fists the slit where loot, diced and unkempt, is hacked out bit by bit.

Welcome to the trail guide for hysterectomy. I am a girl whose inner wilderness is cohabitating with feral beasts. They attach to my uterus. My surgery is a uterectomy. There is no hysteria to remove.

Predarectomies: removal of the predator. It's a goopy, ugly, long procedure. No one visits and flowers do not arrive. There's so much to remove.

THERE'S NO TOMORROW THE SAME AS YESTERDAY

Mothers and fathers lean in doorways to keep anyone from forgetting them. What happens when a personality can't find its way back? Let's say I promise to look for myself in the concerned or deprecating glances of others. Dread filters through the clipped words lost in dwindling lung space. A whirlpool of defiant air is ravenous and terrorizes the mind which wears the fabric of the intestines which now zigzags fear through the furniture.

Inside one house a father helps his son with his vocabulary list. He then heads out to an apartment three streets away. The girl phoned him last week to fix the bathroom window latch. She lives alone. He's a locksmith. He never gets to that, but is able to climb through the tiny enclosure, put on his ski mask and rape the girl. When he arrives home his wife is up. They watch "Cold Case Files." She enjoys the creepy stuff. She cocoons herself under a blanket with him and can't believe the shit people go through.

Kid walks home. Kids walk home. Over and over, shortcut, yes shortcut. Small town, neighborhood, nowhere. "She was still alive at the time," he says. "I thought it was a mannequin. Two legs sticking up out of a fire."

"The kid's body and hair were washed," she said. "Her notebook and schoolbooks were placed neatly next to each hand, as though she would pick them up at any moment."

The detective takes down notes from the officers in charge. She studies the bodies as they line up in her mind at night. Twenty years have diminished yet she will never forget the shadow that split his face in two. A guttural "Shut the fuck up and you won't get killed," spit at her through a specified bass of voice. She starts shaking at the supermarket from the cussing of a random man behind her or two men suddenly arguing on the street.

Body language is stacked against him. He unlocks his arms, puts his palms up on his knees and spreads his legs. His lungs let out a deep breath. Cameras are belching above him. He's not a damn idiot. Learn to plank the sidewalks as if someone is always watching. That's what he knows. The two detectives are playing handball. Let's assume he is the ball in between. A smile, a shrug, or an "I don't recall," are his responses to their slaps. Until they say her name. It's been over a decade. He'd stuffed her in a barrel and left her in a storage space. "Let's take a drive," they say. His hands clench.

She doesn't go to concerts anymore. There's a general avoidance of any place that might jam people in. Sometimes she goes nowhere for weeks. Forgotten in a city is as simple as a month of not returning phone calls or texts. Tolerance has a short fuse. It's a massive history of repeat tracking itself over and over in the annihilation of sanity. She's been to ER and Rehab. Nobody believes her. She opened the door. She let them in. She doesn't have any visible scars and they made her wash herself before they left. The only trial that ever transpired is in her head. The unbelieving faces of her mom and sister haunt her. The detectives nod a bit too often as they write down notes.

And yet, in the dark on certain nights, she hears those grunts again as they tear her apart. The acid-raw ache in her throat and between her thighs slice into a sharpened knife inside her. She can still feel the violent weight of their chests on her body.

And then, sometimes, when the precious light of morning is slanting through her apartment, layering the furniture and rugs in an exquisite sheen, she isn't even sure what exactly happened.

MUSiC AbSORbS WhaT
The BOdy CaN'T

Moments correspond to time in which I can say 'that happened', though equally ineffective as saying I remember. So, sitting on steps I listen to a guy on an acoustic guitar sing "Spill the Wine" and love him, for his face and name are as close as the next coma. A setting within a city that anyone could experience or not.

Songs have the strength to baffle emotions into hangovers of tomorrow with any number of flat notes piled on one another. Some of these songs rack up barely three notes and produce homage to an entire era. So what if a girl languishes over the quivering sentimentality of a few chords. So what? This scourge is what produced an entire life of hovering wants I never clutched. Pained by synapses that flicker on and off like dying light bulbs.

Alright, so add any sample of dialogue here for this guitar strumming boy and the fluttering me who has forgotten his name and face. We say something. There is at least one kiss. We hold hands and feel our genitals move through the palms of our salty hands. A few streetlamps illuminate bony sockets. We study the other's face and wonder who corners the most light.

Blackouts get the most action. Words are recessed and unnecessary. Oh, don't be subtle. It will all be wasted. Those are the first to go. Then the clinging, clutching, and undoing. The pants are at the knees.

Waking up with the sticky stench of sweat and smoking pores saturating me. Always another body and someone I know, but know is a strange thing to call this non-knowledge. It is an acknowledged face rankled with pockmarks and tension. The room stinks of bewilderment and horror. We can't wait to return to our solitary bodies and shower away base, frightened sobriety and whitecap backlash of a night of soiled fingernails scrapping over buttons and zippers to find mottled flesh to spread and douse in.

If only the sun would dry up and stop stabbing me as I walk home alone, with my boots as the landscape and a tune raking through my head.

PLUNGE

Hands behind glass, disarray in head, smell of starched grins, and blur of clocks camouflage time. Who says a castle can't rant out a whole orgy of Bible, room by room? His kids say he slit the Dahlia into a narrative. Peopled by the blue transparency of her veins, pulled up to the skin like someone's lower lip. Slow and deranged martinis guide themselves in clear missiles toward mouths vacant with ruin. The gowned throng spend ample time on upper lids and toenails, depleting energy for the thrill of taunting the hacked starlet.

Prepubescent girls flavor rooms for Man Ray and a swirl with the surreal tracks of hollow. Remixing their angled limbs, terror manifests a floral creature in wait for bulb and burial. Powders blossom in bubbled drinks, rumble distant worlds saturated with adult tongues for hands. Doors lurk sleepy, teeming how little breath is needed to bruise, bleed.

In this castle, mornings never bleary plundered deaths. Flesh and bones zone out, fiddle with zippers and tremors. Damn if somebody isn't leaking horrors of childhood. Men decree motion, play with their trousers and find other men. Girls climb through sabotage, bend into each other.

A table displays the supremacy of defects. Men who dread desperation, load up plates with sausage and ham. Fresh in wrinkles and grimaces they rush to the basement of denial. Girls crumpled with rashed thighs and blazing rectums drink orange juice, huge with the plunge of the sea.

Someone dies. Someone sucks pipes and yells fuck off. Someone lies when police arrive. Someone cries, eats and purges for days. Someone haunts their self and the quiet sky that follows them. Someone has no desire to exist.

UNiFORMiTY of TaSTe

Fingers shudder a soundless strangle, steam thick with the shake of the lens holds crooked images meek with cheap moans entombed within the skin of a hotel as old as its floating daguerreotypes. I chasten as a looter, a blackguard, a scoundrel ghosting money out of the hiss of mourning.

Frail, sucked in by abuse, addiction, they come to my rooms. Stale racks of skin bleed across my beds. Everyone curdles into perversion. A something that dances them like a rag doll, a maid, old as a weaver outskirting deserts.

Some say I bludgeon hundreds. Necks louder than a flock of plundered hens. Can't say I map any of it. It molds towards raucous and the easy snap of the shutter. No need to ask dead bodies to still themselves. Clothes shred askew around them. Adds the mix of dollars in my pocket to the soiled beacon of the buyer's orgasms. Slaughter, hard as acorns, is a marketplace. Sedentary remembrance of the women who scorned them.

My hotel breathes in stock of the city. Ladies temper the whiskers of war inside temperate strangers. Yawn of wives rack the brood of kids, and marriage, men leave behind. Souvenirs are just a part of the ride. Rummaging through the deck like poker cards, the men leave the hotel with their fantasy bound up in a body burdened with a peace it never knew. Branded lifeless in a sepia tone.

ARTERIES MIGRATE TOWARD EXTINCTION

You have three kids, a husband, and an open-coffin vagina. Sister says it dies when you are eight. You throttle caged flesh, vaulted opinions, and the fierce potency of shadows thudding light hungry for habit over forty-two years. Do you know that your sliced throat jawed into three beaming red cherries?

*   *   *   *

When one wife named Frances can't get up from her chair after twenty years of rising to thrash your holey, put on an apron, make meals, and fetch you from the saloon, you find a younger Frances who gutters out like a sailor, irons your brows, and dares the dark to fly you. How do you know you need a nurse? Mom says smoking deflated you into a 6'6", 90 lb. cigarette. They have to gut a 100-year-old oak to pasture your body.

*   *   *   *

Organs pump leaks through your chitchat. Language becomes malignant with pastel nausea. Moves from the shush of nailcare to the bouche of 'how thin are you?' Do they know you have braided your words to signify "your mouth is a muffle of shuffled cards."

Liver racks over a thousand: "Babe, I'll drink whatever shoots my way."

CA-125: normal below 40: your number is over a thousand: "Fuck the roadtrip. I have to pee."

Your face windmills between defending acupuncture and political pantsuits.

* * * *

Can stories actually rearrange continents if they're fondled long enough? Can one become sick of the child molding its plastic haze of saturated assault by parent into caricature? Wider, wider you sully the edges of panic bystanders barely acknowledge. Dare you to hallucinate it off my crotch. Distortion is an autobiography of diagnosis. How many strains of color try to creep through? Your face is an aperture pawing the haggard billows of oozing dignity.

Limp thwarts a captor. Landmines of growling sky shred us piece by piece. Mom surrenders her craving for finger-holds and compliments. She cascades rage that only knows a tightened throat, a word gone ghost, a carcass cough of dormant volcanoes who never find their matted leakage.

Uncle, uncle, you wretched rot-squirrel, how does your family grow? Boy Scout leaders and hetero-breeders who murmur the shadow of blow. Aggravated spits of conversation between awkward, patched silence when Uncle works bolts of rope into Boy Scout specials. Each knot its own anguished plea.

Breastables puff on gang-land rhetoric and spliffs, prison-free of Mom's girdle, yet secondhand silence sods the guzzling beast of appetite and mowed lawns.

Bulk sits beneath its family bush, hoarding depth of exterior. No chance to burrow crazy
when you dominate the cupped sun raking in your placid depravity.

Took off, big sister. "CRAZY" was the dial tone. India was your new home. Dad paid a bill he could never recompense each month. You, sister, shirked your siblings. A dot of a house on the planet of 'nobody will ever know' had grazed the roiling fog of drowned violence. What a family heirloom. A riot of repressed introspection.

A bullet in everyone's head.

squeezed in by despair

The sky absorbs itself into tiny clusters of strangely beaked branches cutting incisions through the veined hiss of tired blue. Step on to the cackle of leaves beneath your shoes. Wallow your way in and out of trees, skeletal tall, old as aches, and smell darkness bleed into each pore. No sense in pretending what the forest hides. Bodies compost history, groan and gnash dust into rich, brazen dirt damp with the guts of wanderers. A multitude of eyes size up the stench of your leeched family tragedies. The caverns of sad, lonely trails deepen across your face. It's okay. You'll never find yourself alone. A pack of swaying columns covered with bark imperceptibly surround you.

Acknowledgments

Thank you to the editors of the following publications where some of these fictions first appeared: *Sleepingfish Magazine, Night Heron Barks, Midway Journal, X-R-A-Y Lit Magazine, No Contact, Heavy Feather Review, Fictive Dream, Flash Fiction Boulevard, Nixes Mate Review, Anti-Heroin Chic, Pioneertown Lit, Lost Balloon, Expat Press, The Rat's Ass Review, Tiny Molecules, Ghost Parachute, Spelk Fiction, New World Writing, Blink-Ink, Z Publishing, Ink in Thirds, Fractured Lit, rk.vr.y, 100 Word Story, Jellyfish Review, Cahoodaloodaling, Drabble Magazine, Thrice Publishing, Crack the Spine Anthology,* and *Best Small Fictions 2021.*

About The Author

Meg Tuite is author of a novel-in-stories, *Domestic Apparition* (San Francisco Bay Press), a short story collection, *Bound By Blue* (Sententia Books), *Meet My Haze* (Big Table Publishing), won the Twin Antlers Collaborative Poetry award from Artistically Declined Press for her poetry collection, *Bare Bulbs Swinging*, as well as five chapbooks of short fiction, flash, poetic prose, and multi-genre writing. She teaches workshops and online classes through *Bending Genres* and is an associate editor at *Narrative Magazine*. Her work has been published in over 600 literary magazines and over fifteen anthologies including *Choose Wisely: 35 Women Up To No Good*. She has been nominated over fifteen times for the Pushcart Prize, won first and second place in *Prick of the Spindle* contest, is a five-time finalist at *Glimmer Train*, a finalist of the Gertrude Stein award, and won third prize in the Bristol Short Story Contest. She is also the editor of eight anthologies, and a story of hers is included in the *Best Small Fictions of 2021*. Her blog: http://megtuite.com.

Other Books by Meg Tuite

Domestic Apparition (San Francisco Bay Press, 2011)

Disparate Pathos (Monkey Puzzle Press, 2011)

Reverberations (Short, Fast, & Deadly Chaps, 2012)

Bound By Blue (Sententia Books, 2013)

Her Skin Is A Costume (Red Bird Chapbooks, 2013)

Bare Bulbs Swinging (Artistically Declined Press, 2014)

Lined Up Like Scars (Flash: The International Short-Short Story Press, 2015)

Grace Notes (Unknown Press, 2015)

Meet My Haze (Big Table Publishing, 2018)

RECENT TITLES FROM UNLIKELY BOOKS

Flight Advice: a fabulary by Tobey Hiller

A Brief Conversation with Consciousness by Marc Vincenz

~getting away with everything by Vincent A. Cellucci and Christopher Shipman

fata morgana by Joel Chace

Typescenes by Rodney A. Brown

Political AF: A Rage Collection by Tara Campbell

The Deepest Part of Dark by Anne Elezabeth Pluto

Swimming Home by Kayla Rodney

Manything by dan raphael

Citizen Relent by Jeff Weddle

The Mercy of Traffic by Wendy Taylor Carlisle

Cantos Poesia by David E. Matthews

Left Hand Dharma: New and Selected Poems by Belinda Subraman

Apocalyptics by C. Derick Varn

Pachuco Skull with Sombrero: Los Angeles, 1970 by Lawrence Welsh

Monolith by Anne McMillen (Second Edition)

When Red Blood Cells Leak by Anne McMillen (Second Edition)

My Hands Were Clean by Tom Bradley (Second Edition)

anonymous gun. by Kurtice Kucheman (Second Edition)

Soy solo palabras but wish to be a city by Leon De la Rósa, illustrated by Gui.ra.ga7 (Second Edition)

www.ingramcontent.com/pod-product-compliance
Lightning Source LLC
Chambersburg PA
CBHW060651260626
47161CB00008B/3087